For the teacher,
GORDON LISH

*I want to cite the names of those
who have my gratitude in respect
of this book—Gardiner Hempel,
Morgan Upton, Rachel Clark, Anderson Ferrell,
Anne Kaiser, Hannah Siegel, Mady Jones,
Liz Darhansoff, Patricia Towers, and,
especially, David Geiser and Nancy Trahms.*

AH

Because grief unites us,
like the locked antlers of moose
who die on their knees in pairs.

—WILLIAM MATTHEWS

Contents

Contents

In a Tub

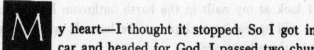

y heart—I thought it stopped. So I got in my car and headed for God. I passed two churches with cars parked in front. Then I stopped at the third because no one else had.

It was early afternoon, the middle of the week. I chose a pew in the center of the rows. Episcopal or Methodist, it didn't make any difference. It was as quiet as a church.

I thought about the feeling of the long missed beat, and the tumble of the next ones as they rushed to fill the space. I sat there—in the high brace of quiet and stained glass—and I listened.

At the back of my house I can stand in the light from the sliding glass door and look out onto the deck. The deck is planted with marguerites and succulents in red clay pots. One of the pots is empty. It is shallow and broad, and filled with water like a birdbath.

My cat takes naps in the windowbox. Her gray chin is powdered with the iridescent dust from butterfly wings. If I tap on the glass, the cat will not look up.

The sound that I make is not food.

When I was a girl I sneaked out at night. I pressed myself to hedges and fitted the shadows of trees. I went to a construction site near the lake. I took a concrete-mixing tub, slid it to the shore, and sat down inside it like a saucer. I would push off from the sand with one stolen oar and float, hearing nothing, for hours.

The birdbath is shaped like that tub.

I look at my nails in the harsh bathroom light. The scare will appear as a ripple at the base. It will take a couple of weeks to see.

I lock the door and run a tub of water.

Most of the time you don't really hear it. A pulse is a thing that you feel. Even if you are somewhat quiet. Sometimes you hear it through the pillow at night. But I know that there is a place where you can hear it even better than that.

Here is what you do. You ease yourself into a tub of water, you ease yourself down. You lie back and wait for the ripples to smooth away. Then you take a deep breath, and slide your head under, and listen for the playfulness of your heart.

Tonight Is a Favor to Holly

A blind date is coming to pick me up, and unless my hair grows an inch by seven o'clock, I am not going to answer the door. The problem is the front. I cut the bangs myself; now I look like Mamie Eisenhower.

Holly says no, I look like Claudette Colbert. But I know why she says that is so I will meet this guy. Tonight is a favor to Holly.

What I'd rather do is what we usually do—mix our rum and Cokes, and drink them on the sand while the sun goes down.

We live the beach life.

Not the one with sunscreen and resort wear. I mean, we just live at the beach. Out the front door is sand. There's the ocean, and we see it every day of the year.

The beach is near the airport—so this town doesn't even have the class L.A. lacks. What it has is airline personnel. For them, it's a twelve-minute shuttle from the concourse home—home meaning a complex of apartments done in fake Spanish Colonial.

It copies the Spanish missions in every direction. But show me the mission with wrought-iron handrails running up the side.

Also, there's a courtyard fountain that splashes onto mosaic tiles. What's irritating is that the tiles were chemically treated to "age" them from the start. What you want to say is, Look, relics are *leftovers*, you know?

The place is called Rancho La Brea, but what it's really called, because of the stewardesses, is Rancho Libido. Inside, the apartments have white sparkle ceilings.

Holly's no stewardess, and neither am I. We're renting month to month while our house is restored from the mud and water damage of the last slide.

Holly sings backup, and sometimes she records. The idea was she would tour, and I'd mostly have the place to myself. But she's not touring. The distribution on her last release was half what she expected. The record company said they had to reorganize their marginal talent, so while Holly looks for another label, she's home nights and my three days off.

Four days a week I drive to La Mirada, to the travel agency where I have a job. It takes me fifty-five minutes to drive one way, and I wish the commute were longer. I like radio personalities, and I like to change lanes. And losing yourself on the freeway is like living at the beach— you're not aware of lapsed time, and suddenly you're there, where it was you were going.

My job fits right in. I *do* nothing, it *pays* nothing, but —you guessed it—it's *better* than nothing.

A sense of humor helps.

The motto of this agency is We Never Knowingly Ruin Your Vacation.

We do two big tours a year, and neither of them now. If I can hold on to it, it's the job I am going to have until my parents die.

I thought I would mind that Holly's always around, but it turns out it's okay. Mornings, we walk to the Casa de Fruta Fruit Stand and Bait Shop. Everything there is the size of something else: strawberries are the size of tomatoes, apples are the size of grapefruits, papayas are the size of watermelons. The one-day sale on cantaloupe is into its third week. We buy enough to fill a blender, plus eggs.

But, back up—because before we get to Casa de Fruta, we have to put on faded Danskins and her ex's boxer shorts, and then be out on the beach watching the lifeguard's jeep drag rakes like combs through the tangled sand.

I like my prints to be the first of the day. Holly's the one who scrapes her blackened feet and curses the tar.

Then the rest of the day happens. Maybe we drain a half tank cruising Holly's territory. Holly calls it research, this looking at men on the more northern sand.

"I'd sooner salt myself away and call it a life," Holly says. "But there's all this research."

Sometimes we check in on Suzy and Hard, the squatters who live at the end of the block. Their aluminum shack has been there for years. The story is he found her at the harbor. She lived from boat to boat, staying with the owner till a fight sent her one berth over.

Suzy has massive sunburned arms and wide hips that jerk unevenly when she walks.

Hard is tall and thin.

His real name is Howard. But Suzy is a slurrer, so it comes out Hard. It seems to fit. Hard has shoulder-length black hair and a mouth as round and mean as a lamprey.

If things are quiet down the block, if the air is thick and still, we float ourselves in the surf. Sometimes a rain begins while we are underwater.

I don't get used to living at the beach, to seeing that wet horizon. It's the edge, the country's aisle seat. But if you made me tell the truth, I'd have to say it's not a good thing. The people who live here, what you hear them say is *I'm supposed to, I'll try, I would have.*

There is no friction here.

It's a kind and buoyant place.

What you forget, living here, is that just because you have stopped sinking doesn't mean you're not still underwater.

Earlier today, Holly answered the phone and took a dinner reservation. Our number is one digit off from Trader Don's, and Holly takes names when she's in a bad mood.

"How many in your party, sir?" she says.

She's afraid I won't go through with what was not my idea. In fact, I am not a person who goes on a date. I don't want to meet men.

I know some already.

We talk about those a lot, and about the ones that Holly knows, too. It's the other thing we do together on my days off.

"You dish, I'll dry," Holly says.

I'll kick things off by calling one a scale model of a man. Holly will say again how if her ex saw a film of the way he had treated her, he would crawl off into the bushes, touch blade, and say goodbye.

Her ex still sends snapshots—pictures of himself on camping trips at the foot of El Capitan or on the shore of Mono Lake. He mounts the pictures on cardboard, which just makes them harder to tear up.

He even stops by when he's in town, and we pretend he's welcome. The two of them, Holly and this ex of hers, sit around and depress each other. They know all of each other's weak points and failings, so they can bring each other down in two-tenths of a second.

When she sees him, Holly says, it's like the sunsets at the beach—once the sun drops, the sand chills quickly. Then it's like a lot of times that were good ten minutes ago and don't count now.

These men, it's not like we don't see them coming. Our intuition is good; the problem is we ignore it.

We keep wanting people to be different.

But who are the people you meet down here?

There are two kinds to choose from: those who are going under and those who aren't moving ahead.

I think Suzy and Hard have more energy than us all. Last night I heard them in the alley. Suzy was screaming. She yelled, "Hard! Look out! You wanna give someone an accident?"

I could see all this from the kitchen. I could see Hard pick up a hubcap and pitch it at Suzy. Suzy squealed and limped away, even though it was her arm he had clipped her on. But then she whirled around and rushed at him. She grabbed his throwing hand and brought it to her mouth. She opened wide to bite. But the scream that followed was hers. The alley is lighted, so I could actually see the white teeth in his hand. Hard stood with his feet apart, and turned sideways. Like a discus-thrower going for the record, he hurled Suzy's dentures onto the roof of Rancho Libido.

I'm hoping this story will break the ice tonight.

Oh, I'll go out with this guy for Holly.

My hair is too short, but I've got teeth in my mouth. I'll be Claudette or Mamie, and he'll be a pretty strange customer himself. He'll be a pimp who's gone through est.

He'll be Hard's brother.

He'll be so dumb there aren't any examples.

All right, I'm smiling when I say this. But the favor I'll expect in return is to not have to do it again.

At least I can look forward to getting home. Holly will be waiting up. She'll make us a Cobra Kiss—that's putting the rum in pomegranate juice. We'll have seconds. Then she'll carry herself to the bedroom like a completed jigsaw puzzle.

I'll get the lights and come after.

The one light I leave on makes the ceiling dance like galaxies. We're hoping next month we can say goodbye to the sparkle ceilings of Rancho Libido. Our old place is cleaning up nicely. Tighter-fitting seals are on the windows, and plywood reinforcements flank the walls. When the next big rain sets off slides, it won't be us at the bottom of the hill, trapped beneath collapsed architecture.

For now, we have our angled beds. Holly's faces east because she claims that facing east wakes you calm and alert. My own goes north to south; unless I'm mistaken, east to west is how they sleep you in your grave.

———

Sometimes we talk about trips. The joke is, the places we think of are beaches, the ones on the folders in my travel office.

What we need to do is move—find some landlocked place where at least half the year the air is cool and dry. It's likely we'll do it, too.

"Sure thing," Holly says. "From the people who brought you Fat Chance."

The truth is, the beach is like excess weight. If we lost it, what would the excuse be then?

A couple of years ago, I *did* go away.

I went east.

A mistake. A few months later the movers packed me up.

There's a thing that happens here, and I thought about it then. Highway One, the coast route, has many scenic lookout points. What happens is that people fall over these cliffs, craning to see to the bottom of them. Sometimes the floor is brush, and sometimes it is rock. It's called going west on Highway One. There is even a club for the people who fall, membership being awarded posthumously.

That's what I thought of when the moving van crashed. It spilled my whole life down a mud ravine, where for two weeks rain kept a crew from hauling it out. Mold embroidered the tablecloths, and newts danced in my shoes.

The message was heavyhanded, but I changed lanes and continued west towards home.

I say an omen that big can be ignored.

Celia Is Back

uck isn't luck," the father told his kids. "Luck is where preparation meets opportunity."

The boy backed up his father's statement. "That's what the *big* winners say," he agreed.

The boy and his sister were entering contests. The kitchen table was littered with forms and the entry blanks off cereal boxes. The boy held a picture of a blue Rolls-Royce, the grand prize in a sweepstakes he was too young to enter.

"Do you think it has to be blue?" he asked. "Do you think I can get it in a different color?"

"You can't drive," the girl said. "So it's a mute point."

She tore a sheet of paper from a legal pad and drew up an affidavit. It promised her the Rolls when her father won it in the sweepstakes next fall. She penciled in a line on the paper for his signature, and a line below that, and titled the second one *Witnessed By*.

The father had time before his weekly appointment, so he poured himself coffee and filled in some of the blanks. In spite of what he said, the father knew he had luck. In the time that he had been home, he had won two prizes. He had won a week for two in Hawaii, airfare included, and a ride in a hot-air balloon.

Sweepstakes were easy, the father explained. There was nothing to guess, no jingle to compose, no skill required at all. You wrote your name and address, then you soaked the paper in water so that it dried stiff and crackly, and was therefore easy for the judge to get a grip on in the bin. You could enter a sweepstakes as often as you liked—you could flood it if the prize or the winning was worth the bother.

The father held his hand up like an Indian saying How. "Remember the Three P's," he told his kids. "Patience, Perseverence, and Postage. The people who win these things know the Three P's."

Contests were different than sweepstakes, he said. You needed talent to win a contest, or at least you needed the knack.

"S-O-S," the father informed. "What you want to remember is: Be Simple, be Original, be Sincere. That's the winning system."

When the sweepstakes entries were completed and stamped, the kids detained their father for the Jell-O pudding contest.

They said, "*Daddy* will help us—Daddy *always* wins!"

"All right," the father said. "But don't make me late for my appointment."

You had to tell the judges why you liked Jell-O pudding. You had to complete the sentence, "I like Jell-O pudding because————."

First, the father looked at what his kids had written down. "It's sincere," he said. "But what about original?" He said that the first thing that popped into their heads would have popped into the heads of other people, too.

The father said, "Think. What is the thing about Jell-O pudding? What is really the thing?"

He paused for so long that the kids looked at each other.

"What?" the girl said.

The father closed his eyes, and leaned back in his chair. He said, "I like Jell-O pudding because I like a good hearty meal after a brisk walk on a winter's day—something to really warm me up."

The boy giggled and the girl giggled.

The father looked confused. "This is the Jell-O pudding contest, isn't that what you said?" he said. "Well, okay then," he said. "I like Jell-O pudding because it has a tough satin finish that resists chipping and peeling. No, no," he said, "I mean, I like Jell-O pudding because it has a fruitier taste. Because it's garden fresh," he said. "Because it goes on dry to protect me from wetness longer. Oh, Jell-O pudding," the father said. "I like it because it's more absorbent than those other brands. Won't chafe or ride up."

He opened his eyes and saw his son leave the room. The sound that had made the father open his eyes was the pen that the boy had thrown to the floor.

"You may already be a winner," the father said.

He closed his eyes again. "You know," he continued, "most pudding makes me edgy. But not *Jell-O* pudding. That's because it has no caffeine. Tastes right—and is built to stay that way.

"Yes, I like Jell-O pudding because it's the one thing to take when you really want to buffricate a headache. Or when you need to mirtilize bad breath, unless you want your bad breath to mirtilize you."

This time the sound that brought him around was the sound of his car keys swinging on their chain. His daughter held the keys. She said, "Daddy, come on. You'll be late."

"That's what I told you, didn't I?" the father said. "I said, 'Don't make me late for my appointment.'"

He followed his daughter out to the car. "Did I tell you the thing about Jell-O?" he said.

His motor skills were not impaired.

He drove slowly, carefully, the girl on the seat beside him. He turned off the freeway onto a wide commercial drive of franchised food and failing business. The place he was going to was blocks away.

A red light stopped him opposite the House of Marlene. There was a handwritten sign in a grimy window. The sign said, *Celia, formerly of Mr. Edward, has rejoined our staff.*

The father's hands relaxed on the wheel.

Celia, he thought.

Celia has come back to make everything okay. The wondrous Celia brings her powers to bear.

The traffic light turned green. Is she really back? he wondered. Is Celia back to stay?

Through the horns going off behind him, through the fists of his daughter beside him, the father stayed stopped.

Everything will be fine, he thought, now that Celia's here.

Nashville Gone to Ashes

fter the dog's cremation, I lie in my husband's bed and watch the Academy Awards for animals. That is not the name of the show, but they give prizes to animals for Outstanding Performance in a movie, on television, or in a commercial. Last year the Schlitz Malt Liquor bull won. The time before that, it was Fred the Cockatoo. Fred won for draining a tinky bottle of "liquor" and then reeling and falling over drunk. It is the best thing on television is what my husband Flea said.

With Flea gone, I watch out of habit.

On top of the warm set is big white Chuck, catching a portion of his four million winks. His tail hangs down and bisects the screen. On top of the dresser, and next to the phone, is the miniature pine crate that holds Nashville's gritty ashes.

Neil the Lion cops the year's top honors. The host says Neil is on location in Africa, but accepting for Neil is his grandson Winston. A woman approaches the stage with a ten-week cub in her arms, and the audience all goes *Awwww*. The home audience, too, I bet. After the cub, they bring the winners on stage together. I figure they must have been sedated—because none of them are biting each other.

I have my own to tend to. Chuck needs tomato juice for his urological problem. Boris and Kirby need brewer's yeast for their nits. Also, I left the vacuum out and the mynah bird is shrieking. Birds think a vacuum-cleaner hose is a snake.

Flea sold his practice after the stroke, so these are the only ones I look after now. These are the ones that always shared the house.

My husband, by the way, was F. Lee Forest, D.V.M. The hospital is right next door to the house.

It was my side that originally bought him the practice. I bought it for him with the applesauce money. My father made an applesauce fortune because *his* way did not use lye to take off the skins. Enough of it was left to me that I had the things I wanted. I bought Flea the practice because I could.

Will Rogers called vets the noblest of doctors because their patients can't tell them what's wrong. The doctor has to reach, and he reaches with his heart.

I think it was that love that I loved. That kind of involvement was reassuring; I felt it would extend to me, as well. That it did not or that it did, but only as much and no more, was confusing at first. I thought, My love is so good, why isn't it calling the same thing back?

Things might have collapsed right there. But the furious care he gave the animals gave me hope and kept me waiting.

I did not take naturally to my husband's work. For instance, I am allergic to cats. For the past twenty years, I have had to receive immunotherapy. These are not pills; they are injections.

Until I was seventeen, I thought a ham was an animal. But I was not above testing a stool sample next door.

I go to the mynah first and put the vacuum cleaner away. This bird, when it isn't shrieking, says only one thing. Flea taught it what to say. He put a sign on its cage that reads *Tell me I'm stupid*. So you say to the bird, "Okay, you're stupid," and the bird says, real sarcastic, "I can talk—can *you fly*?"

Flea could have opened in Vegas with that. But there is no cozying up to a bird.

It will be the first to go, the mynah. The second if you count Nashville.

I promised Flea I would take care of them, and I am. I screened the new owners myself.

Nashville was his favorite. She was a grizzle-colored saluki with lightly feathered legs and Nile-green eyes. You know those skinny dogs on Egyptian pots? Those are salukis, and people worshiped them back then.

Flea acted like he did, too.

He fed that dog dates.

I used to watch her carefully spit out the pit before eating the next one. She sat like a sphinx while he reached inside her mouth to massage her licorice gums. She let him nick tartar from her teeth with his nail.

This is the last time I will have to explain that name. The pick of the litter was named Memphis. They are supposed to have Egyptian names. Flea misunderstood and named his Nashville. A woman back East owns Boston.

At the end of every summer, Flea took Nashville to the Central Valley. They hunted some of the rabbits out of the vineyards. It's called coursing when you use a sight hound. With her keen vision, Nashville would spot a rabbit and point it for Flea to come after. One time she sighted straight up at the sky—and he said he followed her gaze to a plane crossing the sun.

Sometimes I went along, and one time we let Boris hunt, too.

Boris is a Russian wolfhound. He is the size of a float in the Rose Bowl Parade.

He's a real teenager of a dog—if Boris didn't have whiskers, he'd have pimples. He goes through two nyla-bones a week, and once he ate a box of nails.

That's right, a box.

The day we loosed Boris on the rabbits he had drunk a cup of coffee. Flea let him have it, with Half-and-Half, because caffeine improves a dog's trailing. But Boris was so excited, he didn't distinguish his prey from anyone else. He even charged *me*—him, a whole hundred pounds of wolfhound, cranked up on Maxwell House. A sight like that will put a hem in your dress. Now I confine his hunting to the park, let him chase park squab and bald-tailed squirrel.

The first thing F. Lee said after his stroke, and it was three weeks after, was "hanky panky." I believe these words were intended for Boris. Yet Boris was the one who pushed the wheelchair for him. On a flat pave of side-walk, he took a running start. When he jumped, his front paws pushed at the back of the chair, rolling Flea yards ahead with surprising grace.

I asked how he'd trained Boris to do that, and Flea's answer was, "I didn't."

I could love a dog like that, if he hadn't loved him first.

Here's a trick I found for how to finally get some sleep. I sleep in my husband's bed. That way the empty bed I look at is my own.

Cold nights I pull his socks on over my hands. I read in his bed. People still write from when Flea had the column. He did a pet *Q* and *A* for the newspaper. The new doctor sends along letters for my amusement. Here's one I liked—a man thinks his cat is homosexual.

The letter begins, "My cat Frank (not his real name) . . ."

In addition to Flea's socks, I also wear his watch.

A lot of us wear our late-husband's watch.

It's the way we tell each other.

At bedtime, I think how Nashville slept with Flea. She must have felt to him like a sack of antlers. I read about a marriage breaking up because the man let his Afghan sleep in the marriage bed.

I had my own bed. I slept in it alone, except for those times when we needed—not sex—but sex was how we got there.

In the mornings, I am not alone. With Nashville gone, Chuck comes around.

Chuck is a white-haired, blue-eyed cat, one of the few that aren't deaf—not that he comes when he hears you call. His fur is thick as a beaver's; it will hold the tracing of your finger.

Chuck, behaving, is the Nashville of cats. But the most fun he knows is pulling every tissue from a pop-up box of Kleenex. When he gets too rowdy, I slow him down with a comb. Flea showed me how. Scratching the teeth of a comb will make a cat yawn. Then you have him where you want him—any cat, however cool.

Animals are pure, Flea used to say. There is nothing deceptive about them. I would argue: think about cats. They stumble and fall, then quickly begin to wash—I *meant* to do that. Pretense is deception, and cats pretend: Who me? They move in next door where the food is better and meet you in the street and don't know your name, or *their* name.

But in the morning Chuck purrs against my throat, and it feels like prayer.

In the morning is when I pray.

The mailman changed his mind about the bird, and when Mrs. Kaiser came for Kirby and Chuck, I could not find either one. I had packed their supplies in a bag by the door—Chuck's tomato juice and catnip mouse, Kirby's milk of magnesia tablets to clean her teeth.

You would expect this from Chuck. But Kirby is responsible. She's been around the longest, a delicate smallish golden retriever trained by professionals for television work. She was going to get a series, but she didn't grow to size. Still, she can do a number of useless tricks. The one that wowed them in the waiting room next door was Flea putting Kirby under arrest.

"Kirby," he'd say, "I'm afraid you are under arrest." And the dog would back up flush to the wall. "I am going to have to frisk you, Kirb," and she'd slap her paws against the wall, standing still while Flea patted her sides.

Mrs. Kaiser came to visit after her own dog died. When Kirby laid a paw in her lap, Mrs. Kaiser burst into tears.

I thought, God love a dog that hustles.

It is really just that Kirby is head-shy and offers a paw instead of her head to pat. But Mrs. Kaiser remembered the gesture. She agreed to take Chuck, too, when I said he needed a childless home. He gets jealous of kids and has asthma attacks. Myself, I was thinking, with Chuck gone I could have poinsettias and mistletoe in the house at Christmas.

When they weren't out back, I told Mrs. Kaiser I would bring them myself as soon as they showed. She was standing in the front hall talking to Boris. Rather, she was talking *for* Boris.

" 'Oh,' he says, he says, 'what a nice bone,' he says, he says, 'can *I* have a nice bone?' "

Boris walked away and collapsed on a braided rug. " 'Boy,' he says, he says, 'boy, am I bushed.' "

Mrs. Kaiser has worn her husband's watch for years. When she was good and gone, the animals wandered in. Chuck carried a half-eaten chipmunk in his mouth. He dropped it on the kitchen floor, a reminder of the cruelty of a world that lives by food.

After F. Lee's death, someone asked me how I was. I said that I finally had enough hangers in the closet. I don't think that that is what I meant to say. Or maybe it is.

Nashville *died* of *her* broken heart. She refused her food and simply called it quits.

An infection set in.

At the end, I myself injected the sodium pentobarbital.

I felt upstaged by the dog, will you just listen to me!

But the fact is, I think all of us were loved just the same. The love Flea gave to me was the same love he gave them. He did not say to the dogs, I will love you if you keep off the rug. He would love them no matter what they did.

It's what I got, too.

I wanted conditions.

God, how's that for an admission!

My husband said an animal can't disappoint you. I argued this, too. I said, Of course it can. What about the dog who goes on the rug? How does it feel when your efforts to alter behavior come to nothing?

I *know* how it feels.

I would like to think bigger thoughts. But it looks like I don't have a memory of our life that does not include one of the animals.

Kirby still carries in his paper Sunday mornings.

She used to watch while Flea did the crossword puzzle. He pretended to consult her: "I can see why you'd say *dog*, but don't you see—*cat* fits just as well?"

Boris and Kirby still scrap over his slippers. But as Flea used to say, the trouble seldom exceeds their lifespan.

Here we all still are. Boris, Kirby, Chuck—Nashville gone to ashes. Before going to bed I tell the mynah bird she may not be dumb but she's stupid.

Flowers were delivered on our anniversary. The card said the roses were sent by F. Lee. When I called the florist, he said Flea had "love insurance." It's a service they provide for people who forget. You tell the florist the date, and automatically he sends flowers.

Getting the flowers that way had me spooked. I thought I would walk it off, the long way, into town.

Before I left the house, I gave Laxatone to Chuck. With the weather warming up, he needs to get the jump on furballs. Then I set his bowl of Kibbles in a shallow dish of water. I added to the water a spoonful of liquid dish soap. Chuck eats throughout the day; the soapy moat keeps bugs off his plate.

On the walk into town I snapped back into myself.

Two things happened that I give the credit to.

The first thing was the beggar. He squatted on the walk with a dog at his side. He had with him an aged sleeping collie with granular runny eyes. Under its nose was a red plastic dish with a sign that said *Food for dog— donation please.*

The dog was as quiet as any Flea had healed and then rocked in his arms while the anesthesia wore off.

Blocks later, I bought a pound of ground beef.

I nearly ran the distance back.

The two were still there, and a couple of quarters were in the dish. I felt pretty good about handing over the food. I felt good until I turned around and saw the man who was watching me. He leaned against the grate of a closed shoe-repair with an empty tin cup at his feet. He had seen. And I was giving *him—nothing*.

How far do you take a thing like this? I think you take it all the way to heart. We give what we can—that's as far as the heart can go.

This was the first thing that turned me back around to home. The second was just plain rain.

San Francisco

D o you know what I think?

I think it was the tremors. That's what must have done it. The way the floor rolled like bongo boards under our feet? Remember it was you and Daddy and me having lunch? "I guess that's not an earthquake," you said. "I guess you're shaking the table?"

That's when it must have happened. A watch on a dresser, a small thing like that—it must have been shaken right off, onto the floor.

And how would Maidy know? Maidy at the doctor's office? All those years on a psychiatrist's couch and suddenly the couch is *moving*.

Good God, she is on that couch when the big one hits.

Maidy didn't tell you, but you know what her doctor said? When she sprang from the couch and said, "My God, was that an earthquake?"

The doctor said this: "Did it *feel* like an earthquake to you?"

I think we are agreed, you have to look on the light side.

So that's when I think it must have happened. Not that it matters to me. Maidy is the one who wants to know. She thinks she has it coming, being the older daughter. Although where was the older daughter when it happened? Which daughter was it that found you?

When Maidy started asking about your watch, I felt I had to say it. I said, "With the body barely cold?"

Maidy said the body is not the person, that the *essence* is the person, and that the essence leaves the body behind it, along with the body's possessions—for example, its watch?

"Time flies," I said. "Like an arrow.

"*Fruit* flies," I said, and Maidy said, "What?"

"Fruit flies," I said again. "Fruit flies like a banana."

That's how easy it is to play a joke on Maidy.

Remember how easy?

Now Maidy thinks I took your watch. She thinks because I got there first, my first thought was to take it. Maidy keeps asking, "Who took Mama's watch?" She says, "Did *you* take Mama's watch?"

In the Cemetery Where
Al Jolson Is Buried

"T ell me things I won't mind forgetting," she said. "Make it useless stuff or skip it."

I began. I told her insects fly through rain, missing every drop, never getting wet. I told her no one in America owned a tape recorder before Bing Crosby did. I told her the shape of the moon is like a banana—you see it looking full, you're seeing it end-on.

The camera made me self-conscious and I stopped. It was trained on us from a ceiling mount—the kind of camera banks use to photograph robbers. It played us to the nurses down the hall in Intensive Care.

"Go on, girl," she said. "You get used to it."

I had my audience. I went on. Did she know that Tammy Wynette had changed her tune? Really. That now she sings "Stand by Your *Friends*"? That Paul Anka did it too, I said. Does "You're Having *Our* Baby." That he got sick of all that feminist bitching.

"What else?" she said. "Have you got something else?"

Oh, yes.

For her I would always have something else.

"Did you know that when they taught the first chimp to talk, it lied? That when they asked her who did it on the desk, she signed back the name of the janitor. And that when they pressed her, she said she was sorry, that it was really the project director. But she was a mother, so I guess she had her reasons."

"Oh, that's good," she said. "A parable."

"There's more about the chimp," I said. "But it will break your heart."

"No, thanks," she says, and scratches at her mask.

We look like good-guy outlaws. Good or bad, I am not used to the mask yet. I keep touching the warm spot where my breath, thank God, comes out. She is used to hers. She only ties the strings on top. The other ones—a pro by now—she lets hang loose.

We call this place the Marcus Welby Hospital. It's the white one with the palm trees under the opening credits of all those shows. A Hollywood hospital, though in fact it is several miles west. Off camera, there is a beach across the street.

She introduces me to a nurse as the Best Friend. The impersonal article is more intimate. It tells me that *they* are intimate, the nurse and my friend.

"I was telling her we used to drink Canada Dry ginger ale and pretend we were in Canada."

"That's how dumb we were," I say.

"You could be sisters," the nurse says.

So how come, I'll bet they are wondering, it took me so long to get to such a glamorous place? But do they ask?

They do not ask.

Two months, and how long is the drive?

The best I can explain it is this—I have a friend who

worked one summer in a mortuary. He used to tell me stories. The one that really got to me was not the grisliest, but it's the one that did. A man wrecked his car on 101 going south. He did not lose consciousness. But his arm was taken down to the wet bone——and when he looked at it——it scared him to death.

I mean, he died.

So I hadn't dared to look any closer. But now I'm doing it——and hoping that I will live through it.

She shakes out a summer-weight blanket, showing a leg you did not want to see. Except for that, you look at her and understand the law that requires *two* people to be with the body at all times.

"I thought of something," she says. "I thought of it last night. I think there is a real and present need here. You know," she says, "like for someone to do it for you when you can't do it yourself. You call them up whenever you want—like when push comes to shove."

She grabs the bedside phone and loops the cord around her neck.

"Hey," she says, "the end o' the line."

She keeps on, giddy with something. But I don't know with what.

"I can't remember," she says. "What does Kübler-Ross say comes after Denial?"

It seems to me Anger must be next. Then Bargaining, Depression, and so on and so forth. But I keep my guesses to myself.

"The only thing is," she says, "is where's Resurrection? God knows, I want to do it by the book. But she left out Resurrection."

She laughs, and I cling to the sound the way someone dangling above a ravine holds fast to the thrown rope.

"Tell me," she says, "about that chimp with the talking hands. What do they do when the thing ends and the chimp says, 'I don't want to go back to the zoo'?"

When I don't say anything, she says, "Okay—then tell me another animal story. I like animal stories. But not a sick one—I don't want to know about all the seeing-eye dogs going blind."

No, I would not tell her a sick one.

"How about the hearing-ear dogs?" I say. "They're not going deaf, but they are getting very judgmental. For instance, there's this golden retriever in New Jersey, he wakes up the deaf mother and drags her into the daughter's room because the kid has got a flashlight and is reading under the covers."

"Oh, you're killing me," she says. "Yes, you're definitely killing me."

"They say the smart dog obeys, but the smarter dog knows when to disobey."

"Yes," she says, "the smarter anything knows when to disobey. Now, for example."

She is flirting with the Good Doctor, who has just appeared. Unlike the Bad Doctor, who checks the IV drip before saying good morning, the Good Doctor says things like "God didn't give epileptics a fair shake." The Good Doctor awards himself points for the cripples he could have hit in the parking lot. Because the Good

Doctor is a little in love with her, he says maybe a year. He pulls a chair up to her bed and suggests I might like to spend an hour on the beach.

"Bring me something back," she says. "Anything from the beach. Or the gift shop. Taste is no object."

He draws the curtain around her bed.

"Wait!" she cries.

I look in at her.

"Anything," she says, "except a magazine subscription."

The doctor turns away.

I watch her mouth laugh.

What seems dangerous often is not—black snakes, for example, or clear-air turbulence. While things that just lie there, like this beach, are loaded with jeopardy. A yellow dust rising from the ground, the heat that ripens melons overnight—this is earthquake weather. You can sit here braiding the fringe on your towel and the sand will all of a sudden suck down like an hourglass. The air roars. In the cheap apartments on-shore, bathtubs fill themselves and gardens roll up and over like green waves. If nothing happens, the dust will drift and the heat deepen till fear turns to desire. Nerves like that are only bought off by catastrophe.

"It never happens when you're thinking about it," she once observed. "Earthquake, earthquake, earthquake," she said.

"Earthquake, earthquake, earthquake," I said.

Like the aviaphobe who keeps the plane aloft with prayer, we kept it up until an aftershock cracked the ceiling.

That was after the big one in seventy-two. We were in college; our dormitory was five miles from the epicenter. When the ride was over and my jabbering pulse began to slow, she served five parts champagne to one part orange juice, and joked about living in Ocean View, Kansas. I offered to drive her to Hawaii on the new world psychics predicted would surface the next time, or the next.

I could not say that now—next.

Whose next? she could ask.

Was I the only one who noticed that the experts had stopped saying *if* and now spoke of *when*? Of course not; the fearful ran to thousands. We watched the traffic of Japanese beetles for deviation. Deviation might mean more natural violence.

I wanted her to be afraid with me. But she said, "I don't know. I'm just not."

She was afraid of nothing, not even of flying.

I have this dream before a flight where we buckle in and the plane moves down the runway. It takes off at thirty-five miles an hour, and then we're airborne, skimming the tree tops. Still, we arrive in New York on time.

It is so pleasant.

One night I flew to Moscow this way.

She flew with me once. That time she flew with me she ate macadamia nuts while the wings bounced. She knows the wing tips can bend thirty feet up and thirty feet down without coming off. She believes it. She trusts the laws of aerodynamics. My mind stampedes. I can almost accept that a battleship floats when everybody knows steel sinks.

I see fear in her now, and am not going to try to talk her out of it. She is right to be afraid.

After a quake, the six o'clock news airs a film clip of first-graders yelling at the broken playground per their teacher's instructions.

"*Bad* earth!" they shout, because anger is stronger than fear.

But the beach is standing still today. Everyone on it is tranquilized, numb, or asleep. Teenaged girls rub coconut oil on each other's hard-to-reach places. They smell like macaroons. They pry open compacts like clam-shells; mirrors catch the sun and throw a spray of white rays across glazed shoulders. The girls arrange their wet hair with silk flowers the way they learned in *Seventeen*. They pose.

A formation of low-riders pulls over to watch with a six-pack. They get vocal when the girls check their tan lines. When the beer is gone, so are they—flexing their cars on up the boulevard.

Above this aggressive health are the twin wrought-iron terraces, painted flamingo pink, of the Palm Royale. Someone dies there every time the sheets are changed. There's an ambulance in the driveway, so the remaining residents line the balconies, rocking and not talking, one-upped.

The ocean they stare at is dangerous, and not just the undertow. You can almost see the slapping tails of sand sharks keeping cruising bodies alive.

If she looked, she could see this, some of it, from her window. She would be the first to say how little it takes to make a thing all wrong.

There was a second bed in the room when I got back to it!

For two beats I didn't get it. Then it hit me like an open coffin.

She wants every minute, I thought. She wants my life.

"You missed Gussie," she said.

Gussie is her parents' three-hundred-pound narcoleptic maid. Her attacks often come at the ironing board. The pillowcases in that family are all bordered with scorch.

"It's a hard trip for her," I said. "How is she?"

"Well, she didn't fall asleep, if that's what you mean. Gussie's great—you know what she said? She said, 'Darlin', stop this worriation. Just keep prayin', down on your knees'—me, who can't even get out of bed."

She shrugged. "What am I missing?"

"It's earthquake weather," I told her.

"The best thing to do about earthquakes," she said, "is not to live in California."

"That's useful," I said. "You sound like Reverend Ike—'The best thing to do for the poor is not to be one of them.'"

We're crazy about Reverend Ike.

I noticed her face was bloated.

"You know," she said, "I feel like hell. I'm about to stop having fun."

"The ancients have a saying," I said. " 'There are times when the wolves are silent; there are times when the moon howls.' "

"What's that, Navaho?"

"Palm Royale lobby graffiti," I said. "I bought a paper there. I'll read you something."

"Even though I care about nothing?"

I turned to the page with the trivia column. I said, "Did you know the more shrimp flamingo birds eat, the pinker their feathers get?" I said, "Did you know that Eskimos need refrigerators? Do you know *why* Eskimos need refrigerators? Did you know that Eskimos need refrigerators because how else would they keep their food from freezing?"

I turned to page three, to a UPI filler datelined Mexico City. I read her MAN ROBS BANK WITH CHICKEN, about a man who bought a barbecued chicken at a stand down the block from a bank. Passing the bank, he got the idea. He walked in and approached a teller. He pointed the brown paper bag at her and she handed over the day's receipts. It was the smell of barbecue sauce that eventually led to his capture.

The story had made her hungry, she said—so I took the elevator down six floors to the cafeteria, and brought back all the ice cream she wanted. We lay side by side, adjustable beds cranked up for optimal TV-viewing, littering the sheets with Good Humor wrappers, picking toasted almonds out of the gauze. We were Lucy and

Ethel, Mary and Rhoda in extremis. The blinds were closed to keep light off the screen.

We watched a movie starring men we used to think we wanted to sleep with. Hers was a tough cop out to stop mine, a vicious rapist who went after cocktail waitresses.

"This is a good movie," she said when snipers felled them both.

I missed her already.

A Filipino nurse tiptoed in and gave her an injection. The nurse removed the pile of popsicle sticks from the nightstand—enough to splint a small animal.

The injection made us both sleepy. We slept.

I dreamed she was a decorator, come to furnish my house. She worked in secret, singing to herself. When she finished, she guided me proudly to the door. "How do you like it?" she asked, easing me inside.

Every beam and sill and shelf and knob was draped in gay bunting, with streamers of pastel crepe looped around bright mirrors.

"I have to go home," I said when she woke up.

She thought I meant home to her house in the Canyon, and I had to say No, *home* home. I twisted my hands in the time-honored fashion of people in pain. I was supposed to offer something. The Best Friend. I could not even offer to come back.

I felt weak and small and failed.

Also exhilarated.

I had a convertible in the parking lot. Once out of that room, I would drive it too fast down the Coast highway through the crab-smelling air. A stop in Malibu for sangria. The music in the place would be sexy and loud. They'd serve papaya and shrimp and watermelon ice. After dinner I would shimmer with lust, buzz with heat, vibrate with life, and stay up all night.

Without a word, she yanked off her mask and threw it on the floor. She kicked at the blankets and moved to the door. She must have hated having to pause for breath and balance before slamming out of Isolation, and out of the second room, the one where you scrub and tie on the white masks.

A voice shouted her name in alarm, and people ran down the corridor. The Good Doctor was paged over the intercom. I opened the door and the nurses at the station stared hard, as if this flight had been my idea.

"Where is she?" I asked, and they nodded to the supply closet.

I looked in. Two nurses were kneeling beside her on the floor, talking to her in low voices. One held a mask over her nose and mouth, the other rubbed her back in slow circles. The nurses glanced up to see if I was the doctor—and when I wasn't, they went back to what they were doing.

"There, there, honey," they cooed.

On the morning she was moved to the cemetery, the one where Al Jolson is buried, I enrolled in a "Fear of

Flying" class. "What is your worst fear?" the instructor asked, and I answered, "That I will finish this course and still be afraid."

I sleep with a glass of water on the nightstand so I can see by its level if the coastal earth is trembling or if the shaking is still me.

What do I remember?

I remember only the useless things I hear—that Bob Dylan's mother invented Wite-Out, that twenty-three people must be in a room before there is a fifty-fifty chance two will have the same birthday. Who cares whether or not it's true? In my head there are bath towels swaddling this stuff. Nothing else seeps through.

I review those things that will figure in the retelling: a kiss through surgical gauze, the pale hand correcting the position of the wig. I noted these gestures as they happened, not in any retrospect—though I don't know why looking back should show us more than looking *at*.

It is just possible I will say I stayed the night.

And who is there that can say that I did not?

I think of the chimp, the one with the talking hands.

In the course of the experiment, that chimp had a baby. Imagine how her trainers must have thrilled when the mother, without prompting, began to sign to her newborn.

Baby, drink milk.

Baby, play ball.

And when the baby died, the mother stood over the body, her wrinkled hands moving with animal grace, forming again and again the words: Baby, come hug, Baby, come hug, fluent now in the language of grief.

for Jessica Wolfson

Beg, Sl Tog, Inc, Cont, Rep

The mohair was scratchy, the stria too bulky, but the homespun tweed was right for a small frame. I bought slate-blue skeins softened with flecks of pink, and size-10 needles for a sweater that was warm but light. The pattern I chose was a two-tone V-neck with an optional six-stitch cable up the front. Pullovers mess the hair, but I did not want to buttonhole the first time out.

From a needlework book, I learned to cast on. In the test piece, I got the gauge and correct tension. Knit and purl came naturally, as though my fingers had been rubbed in spiderwebs at birth. The sliding of the needles was as rhythmic as water.

Learning to knit was the obvious thing. The separation of tangled threads, the working-together of raveled ends into something tangible and whole—this *mending* was as confounding as the groom who drives into a stop sign on the way to his wedding. Because symptoms mean just what they are. What about the woman whose empty hand won't close because she cannot grasp that her child is gone?

"Would you get me a Dr Pep, gal, and would you turn up the a-c?"

I put down my knitting. In the kitchen I found some sugar-free, and took it, with ice, to Dale Anne. It was August. Air-conditioning lifted her hair as she pressed the button on the Niagara bed. Dr. Diamond insisted she have it the last month. She was also renting a swivel TV table and a vibrating chaise—the Niagara adjustable home.

When the angle was right, she popped a Vitamin E and rubbed the oil where the stretch marks would be.

I could be doing this, too. But I had had the procedure instead. That was after the father had asked me, Was I sure? To his credit, he meant—sure that I *was*, not sure was it he. He said he had never made a girl pregnant before. He said that he had never even made a girl late.

I moved in with Dale Anne to help her near the end. Her husband is often away—in a clinic or in a lab. He studies the mind. He is not a doctor yet, but we call him one by way of encouragement.

I had picked up a hank of yarn and was winding it into a ball when the air-conditioner choked to a stop.

Dale Anne sighed. "I will *cook* in this robe. Would you get me that flowered top in the second drawer?"

While I looked for the top, Dale Anne twisted her hair and held it tight against her head. She took one of my double-pointed six-inch needles and wove it in and out of her hair, securing the twist against her scalp. With the hair off her face, she looked wholesome and very young—"the person you would most like to go camping with if you couldn't have sex," is how she put it.

I turned my back while Dale Anne changed. She was as modest as I was. If the house caught fire one night, we would both die struggling to hook brassieres beneath our gowns.

I went back to my chair, and as I did, a sensational cramp snapped me over until I was nearly on the floor.

"Easy, gal—what's the trouble?" Dale Anne started out of bed to come see.

I said it sometimes happens since the procedure, and Dale Anne said, "Let's not talk about that for at *least* ten years."

I could not think of what to say to that. But I didn't have to. The front door opened, earlier than it usually did. It was Dr. Diamond, home from the world of spooks and ghosts and loony bins and Ouija boards. I knew that a lack of concern for others was a hallmark of mental illness, so I straightened up and said, after he'd kissed his pregnant wife, "You look hot, Dr. Diamond. Can I get you a drink?"

I buy my materials at a place in the residential section. The owner's name is Ingrid. She is a large Norwegian woman who spells needles "kneedles." She wears sample knits she makes up for the class demonstrations. The vest she wore the day before will be hanging in the window.

There are always four or five women at Ingrid's round oak table, knitting through a stretch they would not risk alone.

Often I go there when I don't need a thing. In the small back room that is stacked high with pattern books, I can sift for hours. I scan the instructions abbreviated like musical notation: *K10, sl 1, K2 tog, psso, sl 1, K10 to end.* I feel I could *sing* these instructions. It is compression of language into code; your ability to decipher it makes you privy to the secrets shared by Ingrid and the women at the round oak table.

In the other room, Ingrid tells a customer she used to knit two hundred stitches a minute.

I scan the French and English catalogues, noting the longer length of coat. There is so much to absorb on each visit.

Mary had a little lamb, I am humming when I leave the shop. *Its feet were—its fleece was white as wool.*

Dale Anne wanted a nap, so Dr. Diamond and I went out for margaritas. At La Rondalla, the colored lights on the Virgin tell you every day is Christmas. The food arrives on manhole covers and mariachis fill the bar. Dr. Diamond said that in Guadalajara there is a mariachi college that turns out mariachis by the classful. But I could tell that these were not graduates of even mariachi high school.

I shooed the serenaders away, but Dr. Diamond said they meant well.

Dr. Diamond likes for people to mean well. He could be president of the Well-Meaning Club. He has had a buoyant feeling of fate since he learned Freud died the day he was born.

He was the person to talk to, all right, so I brought up the stomach pains I was having for no bodily reason that I could think of.

"You know how I think," he said. "What is it you can't stomach?"

I knew what he was asking.

"Have you thought about how you will feel when Dale Anne has the baby?" he asked.

With my eyes, I wove strands of tinsel over the Blessed Virgin. That was the great thing about knitting, I thought—everything was fiber, the world a world of natural resource.

"I thought I would burn that bridge when I come to it," I said, and when he didn't say anything to that, I said, "I guess I will think that there is a mother who *kept* hers."

"*One* of hers might be more accurate," Dr. Diamond said.

I arrived at the yarn shop as Ingrid turned over the *Closed* sign to *Open*. I had come to buy Shetland wool for a Fair Isle sweater. I felt nothing would engage my full attention more than a pattern of ancient Scottish symbols and alternate bands of delicate design. Every stitch in every color is related to the one above, below, and to either side.

I chose the natural colors of Shetland sheep—the chalky brown of the Moorit, the blackish brown of the black sheep, fawn, gray, and pinky beige from a mixture of Moorit and white. I held the wool to my nose, but Ingrid said it was fifty years since the women of Fair Isle dressed the yarn with fish oil.

She said the yarn came from Sheep Rock, the best pasture on Fair Isle. It is a ten-acre plot that is four hundred feet up a cliff, Ingrid said. "Think what a man has to go through to harvest the wool."

I was willing to feel an obligation to the yarn, and to the hardy Scots who supplied it. There was heritage there, and I could keep it alive with my hands.

Dale Anne patted capers into a mound of raw beef, and spread some onto toast. It was not a pretty sight. She offered some to me, and I said not a chance. I told her Johnny Carson is someone else who won't go near that. I said, "Johnny says he won't eat steak tartare because he has seen things hurt worse than that get better."

"Johnny was never pregnant," Dale Anne said.

When the contractions began, I left a message with the hospital and with Dr. Diamond's lab. I turned off the air-conditioner and called for a cab.

"Look at you," Dale Anne said.

I told her I couldn't help it. I get rational when I panic.

The taxi came in minutes.

"Hold on," the driver said. "I know every bump in these roads, and I've never been able to miss one of them."

Dale Anne tried to squeeze my wrist, but her touch was weightless, as porous as wet silk.

"When this is over . . ." Dale Anne said.

When the baby was born, I did not go far. I sublet a place on the other side of town. I filled it with patterns and needles and yarn. It was what I did in the day. On a good day, I made a front and two sleeves. On a bad day, I ripped out stitches from neck to hem. For variety,

I made socks. The best ones I made had beer steins on the sides, and the tops spilled over with white angora foam.

I did not like to work with sound in the room, not even the sound of a fan. Music slowed me down, and there was a great deal to do. I planned to knit myself a mailbox and a car, perhaps even a dog and a lead to walk him.

I blocked the finished pieces and folded them in drawers.

Dr. Diamond urged me to exercise. He called from time to time, looking in. He said exercise would set me straight, and why not have some fun with it? Why not, for example, tap-dancing lessons?

I told him it would be embarrassing because the rest of the class would be doing it right. And with all the knitting, there wasn't time to dance.

Dale Anne did not look in. She had a pretty good reason not to.

The day I went to see her in the hospital, I stopped at the nursery first. I saw the baby lying face down. He wore yellow duck-print flannels. I saw that he was there —and then I went straight home.

That night the dreams began. A giant lizard ate people from the feet upwards, swallowing the argyles on the first bite, then drifting into obscurity like a ranger of forgotten death. I woke up remembering and, like a chameleon, assumed every shade of blame.

Asleep at night, I went to an elegant ball. In the center of the dance floor was a giant aquarium. Hundreds of goldfish swam inside. At a sign from the bandleader, the tank was overturned. Until someone tried to dance on the fish, the floor was aswirl with gold glory.

Dr. Diamond told a story about the young daughter of a friend. The little girl had found a frog in the yard. The frog appeared to be dead, so her parents let her prepare a burial site—a little hole surrounded by pebbles. But at the moment of the lowering, the frog, which had only been stunned, kicked its legs and came to.

"Kill him!" the girl had shrieked.

I began to take walks in the park. In the park, I saw a dog try to eat his own shadow, and another dog—I am sure of it—was herding a stand of elms. I stopped telling people how handsome their dogs were; too many times what they said was, "You want him?"

When the weather got nicer, I stayed home to sit for hours.

I had accidents. Then I had bigger ones. But the part that hurt was never the part that got hurt.

The dreams came back and back until they were just—again. I wished that things would stay out of sight the way they did in mountain lakes. In one that I know, the water is so cold, gas can't form to bring a corpse to the surface. Although you would not want to think about the bottom of the lake, what you can say about it is—the dead stay down.

Around that time I talked to Dr. Diamond.

The point that he wanted to make was this: that conception was not like walking in front of traffic. No matter how badly timed, it was, he said, an affirmation of life.

"You have to believe me here," he said. "Do you see that this is true? Do you know this about yourself?"

"I do and I don't," I said.

"You do and you *do*," he said.

I remembered when another doctor made the news. A young retarded boy had found his father's gun, and while the family slept, he shot them all in bed. The police asked the boy what he had done. But the boy went mute. He told them nothing. Then they called in the doctor.

"We know *you* didn't do it," the doctor said to the boy, "but tell me, did the *gun* do it?"

And yes, the boy was eager to tell him just what that gun had done.

I wanted the same out, and Dr. Diamond wouldn't let me have it.

"Dr. Diamond," I said, "I am giving up."

"Now you are ready to begin," he said.

I thought of Andean alpaca because that was what I planned to work up next. The feel of that yarn was not the only wonder—there was also the name of it: Alpaquita Superfina.

Dr. Diamond was right.

I was ready to begin.

Beg, sl tog, inc, cont, rep.

Begin, slip together, increase, continue, repeat.

Dr. Diamond answered the door. He said Dale Anne had run to the store. He was leaving, too, flying to a conference back East. The baby was asleep, he said, I should make myself at home.

I left my bag of knitting in the hall and went into

Dale Anne's kitchen. It had been a year. I could have looked in on the baby. Instead, I washed the dishes that were soaking in the sink. The scouring pad was steel wool waiting for knitting needles.

The kitchen was filled with specialized utensils. When Dale Anne couldn't sleep she watched TV, and that's where the stuff was advertised. She had a thing to core tomatoes—it was called a Tomato Shark—and a metal spaghetti wheel for measuring out spaghetti. She had plastic melon-ballers and a push-in device that turned ordinary cake into ladyfingers.

I found pasta primavera in the refrigerator. My fingers wanted to knit the cold linguini, laying precisely cabled strands across the oily red peppers and beans.

Dale Anne opened the door.

"*Look* out, gal," she said, and dropped a shopping bag on the counter.

I watched her unload ice cream, potato chips, carbonated drinks, and cake.

"It's been a long time since I walked into a market and expressed myself," she said.

She turned to toss me a carton of cigarettes.

"Wait for me in the bedroom," she said. "*West Side Story* is on."

I went in and looked at the color set. I heard the blender crushing ice in the kitchen. I adjusted the contrast, then Dale Anne handed me an enormous peach daiquiri. The goddamn thing had a tide factor.

Dale Anne left the room long enough to bring in the take-out chicken. She upended the bag on a plate and picked out a leg and a wing.

"I like my dinner in a bag and my life in a box," she said, nodding toward the TV.

We watched the end of the movie, then part of a lame detective program. Dale Anne said the show *owed* Nielsen four points, and reached for the *TV Guide*.

"Eleven-thirty," she read. "*The Texas Whiplash Massacre*: Unexpected stop signs were their weapon."

"Give me that," I said.

Dale Anne said there was supposed to be a comet. She said we could probably see it if we watched from the living room. Just to be sure, we pushed the couch up close to the window. With the lights off, we could see everything without it seeing us. Although both of us had quit, we smoked at either end of the couch.

"Save my place," Dale Anne said.

She had the baby in her arms when she came back in. I looked at the sleeping child and thought, Mercy, Land Sakes, Lordy Me. As though I had aged fifty years. For just a moment then I wanted nothing that I had and everything I did not.

"He told his first joke today," Dale Anne said.

"What do you mean he told a joke?" I said. "I didn't think they could talk."

"Well, he didn't really *tell* a joke—he poured his orange juice over his head, and when I started after him, he said, 'Raining?' "

" 'Raining?' That's what he said? The kid is a genius," I told Dale Anne. "What Art Linkletter could do with this kid."

Dale Anne laid him down in the middle of the couch, and we watched him or watched the sky.

"What a gyp," Dale Anne said at dawn.

There had not been a comet. But I did not feel cheated, or even tired. She walked me to the door.

The knitting bag was still in the hall.

"Open it later," I said. "It's a sweater for him."

But Dale Anne had to see it then.

She said the blue one matched his eyes and the camel one matched his hair. The red would make him glow, she said, and then she said, "Help me out."

Cables had become too easy; three more sweaters had pictures knitted in. They buttoned up the front. Dale Anne held up a parade of yellow ducks.

There were the Fair Isles, too—one in the pattern called Tree of Life, another in the pattern called Hearts.

It was an excess of sweaters—a kind of precaution, a rehearsal against disaster.

Dale Anne looked at the two sweaters still in the bag. "Are you really okay?" she said.

The worst of it is over now, and I can't say that I am glad. Lose that sense of loss—you have gone and lost something else. But the body moves toward health. The mind, too, in steps. One step at a time. Ask a mother who has just lost a child, How many children do you have? "Four," she will say, "—three," and years later, "Three," she will say, "—four."

It's the little steps that help. Weather, breakfast, crossing with the light—sometimes it is all the pleasure I can bear to sleep, and know that on a rack in the bath, damp wool is pinned to dry.

Dale Anne thinks she would like to learn to knit. She measures the baby's crib and I take her over to

Ingrid's. Ingrid steers her away from the baby pastels, even though they are machine-washable. Use a pure wool, Ingrid says. Use wool in a grown-up shade. And don't boast of your achievements or you'll be making things for the neighborhood.

On Fair Isle there are only five women left who knit. There is not enough lichen left growing on the island for them to dye their yarn. But knitting machines can't produce their designs, and they keep on, these women, working the undyed colors of the sheep.

I wait for Dale Anne in the room with the patterns. The songs in these books are like lullabies to me.

K tog rem st. Knit together remaining stitches.

Cast off loosely.

Going

There is a typo on the hospital menu this morning. They mean, I think, that the pot roast tonight will be served with buttered noodles. But what it says here on my breakfast tray is that the pot roast will be *severed* with buttered noodles.

This is not a word you want to see after flipping your car twice at sixty per and then landing side-up in a ditch.

I did not spin out on a stretch of highway called Blood Alley or Hospital Curve. I lost it on flat dry road —with no other car in sight. Here's why: in the desert I like to drive through binoculars. What I like about it is that things are two ways at once. Things are far away and close with you still in the same place.

In the ditch, things were also two ways at once. The air was unbelievably hot and my skin was unbelievably cold.

"Son," the doctor said, "you shouldn't be alive."

The impact knocked two days out of my head, but all you can see is the cut on my chin. I total a car and get twenty stitches that keep me from shaving.

It's a good thing, too, that that is all it was. This hospital place, this clinic—it is not your City of Hope. The instruments don't come from a first-aid kit, they come from a toolbox. It's the desert. The walls of this room are not rose-beige or sanitation-plant green. The walls are the color of old chocolate going chalky at the edges.

And there's a worm smell.

Though I could be mistaken about the smell.

I'm given to olfactory hallucinations. When my parents' house was burning to the ground, I smelled smoke three states away.

Now I smell worms.

The doctor wants to watch me because I knocked my head. So I get to miss a few days of school. It's okay with me. I believe that ninety-nine percent of what anyone does can effectively be postponed. Anyway, the accident was a learning experience.

You know—pain teaches?

One of the nurses picked it up from there. She was bending over my bed, snatching pebbles of safety glass out of my hair. "What do we learn from this?" she asked.

It was like that class at school where the teacher talks about Realization, about how you could realize something big in a commonplace thing. The example he gave—and the liar said it really happened—was that once while drinking orange juice, he'd realized he would be dead someday. He wondered if we, his students, had had similar "realizations."

Is he kidding? I thought.

Once I cashed a paycheck and I realized it wasn't enough.

Once I had food poisoning, and realized I was trapped inside my body.

What interests me now is this memory thing. Why two *days*? Why *two* days? The last I know is not getting carded in a two-shark bar near the Bonneville flats. The bartender served me tequila and he left the bottle out. He asked me where I was going, and I said I was just going. Then he brought out a jar with a scorpion in it. He showed me how a drop of tequila on its tail makes a scorpion sting itself to death.

What happened after that?

Maybe those days will come back and maybe they will not. In the meantime, how's this: I can't even remember all I've forgotten.

I do remember the accident, though. I remember it was like the binoculars. You know—two ways? It was fast and it was slow. It was both.

The pot roast wasn't bad. I ate every bit of it. I finished the green vegetables and the citrus vegetables too.

Now I'm waiting for the night nurse. She takes a blood pressure about this time. You could call this the high point of my day. That's because this nurse makes every other woman look like a sex-change. Unfortunately, she's in love with the Lord.

But she's a sport, this nurse. When I can't sleep she brings in the telephone book. She sits by my bed and we look up funny names. Calliope Ziss and Maurice Pancake live in this very community.

I like a woman in my room at night.

The night nurse smells like a Christmas candle.

After she leaves the room, for a short time the room is like when she was here. She is not here, but the idea of her is.

It's not the same—but it makes me think of the night my mother died. Three states away, the smell in my room was the smell of the powder on her face when she kissed me good-night—the night she wasn't there.

Pool Night

Pool Night

T his time it happened with fire. Just the way it
happened before, the time it happened with
water. Someone was losing everything—to water, to fire
—and not trying not to.

Maybe I wasn't losing everything. But I didn't try
to save it. That is what makes it like the first time. They
had to lead me out of the house, and not because I didn't
know my way out in the smoke.

The first time, no one said anything. Or we talked
about everything but. It was twenty-eight years since the
river topped its banks, all that time since a flood skunked
the reservoir and washed out people's homes.

We watched the water come, when it did. From patios
late at night, the neighborhood watched the water move.
A flash of light like strobe light would go off on the
ground as the watery debris snapped a high tension tower.
When the wires touched the water, that part of town
went black. This was the thing we watched—the city
going dark along the path of the flood.

It was not supposed to reach us.

And then it did.

Evacuation was calm and quick, except for Dr. Winton. Dr. Winton drank down most of his liquor cabinet

and stared at the Red Cross volunteers who put their van in park and went in and hauled him out.

Most of us saw that happen. But during the days of cleanup it was not what anyone mentioned. We talked about the racehorses loose from Centennial Track, how they had cantered over lawns and stumbled on buried sprinkler heads. Indoors were rolls of wet toilet paper swelling on bathroom rods. We found letters, and water had washed off the ink.

We talked about Bunny Winton, who ordered a new living room the first morning after. She said she was happy to see her armchairs go, the padded arms cat-scratched down to cotton batting.

"You open up or you shut down," Bunny said, and went out and got her hair styled new.

Film crews photographed the swim team at the Club. They were lined up by the snack bar, waiting to get a tetanus shot so they could shovel mud. Bunny made the nightly news; the vidifont spelled out VICTIM on her chest.

They showed her in a tree wrapping washcloths around a branch so that the wet bent wood would not squeak against the roof.

The first time was fifteen years ago, on what was, or on what would have been, Pool Night.

"It's all in the mouth," he said, and showed me again and again. Grey said, "If the mouth is relaxed, the person looks good."

We were looking at pictures of ourselves and family. The looking was my mother's idea—my mother, who was the thoughtful one. Here's what my mother thought of when she heard that Bunny Winton had lost her photograph album: she put me to work on ours. Grey came over to help me—at her invitation, of course.

Grey was Bunny and the Doctor's son, the child they could not now watch grow up in snapshots, page after page. Until my mother remembered that he grew up in ours. We would pull every picture that included Grey Winton, print up another, and present a new album to his grateful parents.

Grey was a junior lifeguard at the pool. He tanned to the color of the corn flakes he ate each morning, and I knew girls who saved his chewed gum.

Grey was the only boy excused from working cleanup. That was the week he was under observation.

He and my brother were Aquazaniacs.

They trained with a coach to do slapstick acrobatics off the high dive at the pool. There were six Aquazaniacs in 1890's stripes who hurled themselves into the water in syncopated ways. Grey would stand on my brother's shoulders and together they dove as The Twelve-Foot Man.

In the pratfall sport of Clown Diving, the Walk-Around Gainer is a popular stunt. This is where you run to the end of the board and then keep on running, out in the air, a cartoon, so fast you flip over backwards.

"Put gravity at your service," is how they said they did it.

But during rehearsal, Grey candied out. He hit his head on the board coming down. It would have kept him from diving on Pool Night, if we had had Pool Night. But the rain date gave him time to try to perfect the Fire Dive.

In the album there were pictures of Grey in water. The first one was in our bathtub, playing Stormy Ocean with my brother as a baby. Later, they pole a raft across a lake, poking an oar at snapping turtles. There's a picture of the three of us on skates, on ice. Around my neck I wear snowballs of rabbit fur on black velvet cord. The pictures that follow show the boys pulling the snowballs off, then coming from behind, the velvet rope stretched out tight—a garrote.

Some of the photographs were Polaroid ones. They were faded, but the fugitive images remained. Emulsion on others had turned metallic bronze; the snapshots held deep tarnish, like a mirror.

There were quite a few pictures of Bunny, too. With the unphotogenic's eagerness to pose, she increased her chances of the one good shot that would let her relax, having proof at last that she had once looked good, just once.

The Doctor couldn't make it to the picnics or to the skating—so he didn't show up in the pictures, either. The effect was of him saying after the flood: What I lose will always be lost.

"His problem is the past," Grey said about his father. "He says only do things you have done before and liked. Whereas me, what's *coming* is the thing I'm looking out for."

I thought the present was the safer bet. We can only

die in the future, I thought; right now we are always alive.

Grey trusted water. He continued to trust it after the flood. He believed it would save him, and he counted on this for the Fire Dive.

I saw him do it once, which is all the times he did it.

When the swimming pool was filtered and rechlorinated, he carried a can of gasoline to the high board. He wore a sweatshirt with a hood and matching drawstring pants. He dove into the water with the top and bottoms on, then pulled himself out by the ladder on the side. It was night, and I had my camera ready.

He sprinkled his wet clothes with gasoline as though he were watering plants. He said wet cloth would pull the fuel away from his skin.

He said to imagine this: that the moment he hit the water aflame, when he made this dive on the next Pool Night, that's when he would have a cannon go off!

Then he struck a lighter and he lit himself up good.

I got it all on film—the human torch, the flaming spiral twists that he scripted in the air, the hiss of reclaimed life when the water took him in.

It only lasted seconds. It seemed an extravagant risk, and that is how I put it.

He said, "I made those seconds live."

I took one more picture that night. It was after Grey had walked me home. He found a box of photograph corners, the black stick-on kind that frame the picture on the page. He opened up our album, pasted four of them in place.

It was *Grey* who took the picture; the picture he took was of me. It was candid—I wasn't posed—and the instant, the Polaroid, is what he used. When the blank square of film emerged from the camera, he tore it off and slipped it in the corners on the page, and then he closed the album cover before the image could develop.

That picture is something I lost in the fire.

One thing smoke does is lower your voice. It did not sound like me, thanking the firefighters. I said thanks, but I did not feel grateful. I stood aside and watched, breathing the tarry air. I watched myself lose all that I was losing, and I knew why Dr. Winton had stayed inside his house.

I know about this now.

I know that homes burn and that you should think what to save before they start to. Not because, in the heat of it, everything looks as valuable as everything else. But because nothing looks worth the bother, not even your life.

Three Popes
Walk into a Bar

ydney Lawton Square is a park for a transient
population; there are no benches. You can walk
it end to end in minutes. The architect for the Gateway
Condominiums squeezed it in between the barbecue place
and the parking garage. You would put quotes around
this "park" the way you might send traffic fines to the
Hall of "Justice." But this feeble attempt at nature is
walking distance from the club—so that's where I meet
Wesley, at the Fountain of Four Seasons.

The fountain yields dead earthworms, not coins;
the worms outnumber pull-tabs, cigarettes, and leaves.
At the nearby north entrance to the square there is a
faded brick arch with a bronzelike plaque that says
HISTORICAL SITE. All of it is contrived to suggest that
something was once there, but none of it tells you what.

Wesley calls out "Ahoy," so I know he has made up
his mind.

"You think it's a crime to change your mind?" he
says. "Just because you are able to do a thing doesn't
mean that's what you have to do, does it? Because I
could but I don't want to," he says as we walk the
tarmac path.

He is talking about performing. He's still funny, and
he wants to stop.

"I could keep on," he says, "and you know what

I'd have to show for it? Ten percent liver function and a felony in my bed."

"I think what counts is timing," I say. "As long as you try your first choice first."

Three popes walk into a bar.

A guy in the airport Clipper Club recognized Wesley and bet him he couldn't get a punchline out of it. They boarded a plane in Honolulu; Wesley had the five hours to San Francisco to make it a joke. *Three popes walk into a bar.* He lost money on this, but I didn't ask how much. Coming off a tour he is sick with foreign germs. I met him at the gate and drove him straight to the club. It's what Eve usually did, but she delegated to me. Eve Grant is Wesley Grant's future former wife.

"Eve cabled the hotel that she's coming tonight," Wesley said. "But she won't laugh."

"You won't hear her not laughing over the six hundred other people," I said. "You're sold out."

"But I always know. You *know.* She wants me to buy a boat, is all. After, of course, I have stopped performing."

"What's it to her?" I said. "She's leaving you."

"Or not," Wesley said. "Maybe she's not leaving if I buy the boat."

"That doesn't put you on the spot or anything."

"You talk to her tonight," he said.

About Eve Grant, Wesley has said that he married the most beautiful woman he ever saw and learned the irrelevance of beauty.

He met her at a club where she danced topless. She told him that Wesley was the name of the first monkey in space. She told him how NASA used that Wesley up and then abandoned him to an animal shelter for destruction. Then a group of women kidnapped that Wesley and took him to a zoo, where he lived out his life in comfort.

Wesley knew the monkey's name was Steve, but thought it was sweet of her to say otherwise.

With Wesley's encouragement, Eve stopped dancing and pursued a career in journalism. She thought she would be a natural at it because people always wanted to talk to her. She wrote an article on spec for the Sunday paper and had it returned six weeks later. Wesley asked the editor what was wrong with it, wasn't it boring enough? Then he cashed a favor with a publicist and got Eve a job at a fan-zine doing a monthly column on vanished TV actors. The column was called "Where Are They Now?" but we all called it "Why Aren't They Dead?"

Wesley signaled the waitress and placed a special order. In a moment, she returned with a bowl of canned peach halves. Wesley took a bottle of Romilar cough suppressant from his coat pocket and poured most of it into the bowl.

"I really admire you," I told him. "I couldn't go out there and make people laugh if *I* were sick."

"Don't be silly," he said. "You couldn't do it if you were well."

He forced down the reddened peaches.

"But I'll tell you what you *can* do. You can tickle me," he said.

Eve usually did that, too. His grandmother started it when he was a boy. She used to tickle Wesley beyond fun, he said, until he felt trapped and helpless and would have cried except that he learned to give in to it, and at that moment felt relief and calm move in.

It is this tickling and giving in that makes him funny, he thinks. Like every kind of recovery, comedy demands surrender.

Wesley cleared away the chairs and squared off in front of me. At the signal I dove at his belt.

I get something out of this, too.

The club manager's office was open and empty, so we took a couple of drinks in and closed the door. Wesley scanned the shelves of video cassettes, pulled one out and popped it into the deck. He joined me on the couch.

It was a tape of every low-budget commercial he had made for local affiliate stations. This, Wesley said, is comedy.

The tape kicked in and there he was in suit and tie for the Cherry Hills Shopping Mall over in the East Bay.

"Tell me when it's safe," he said, and covered his eyes with a hand.

On screen, he said, "That's Cherry Hills, between the MacArthur and the Nimitz. MacArthur and Nimitz— both fine men, both fine freeways."

"Oh, I hate myself," he moaned.

The machine sizzled with static.

"This next one is Eve's favorite."

The product was a deep-penetrating epoxy sealer that you pumped into cracked cement to bind it into one integral piece again. The homeowner in the background eyeing his cracked sidewalk was Wesley's former partner, Larry Banks. They split up a couple of years ago when Banks ran for mayor on the campaign platform, "Anything You Want."

The machine jammed on the tagline, "Cement cracks, this we know."

Wesley turned off the machine and opened the door. He asked the waitress for vodka.

"I tell you about the night I met Banks?" he said. "My manager brought him to watch me work. Then after the show we all go to this Polynesian place to get stewed. Banks, he was just starting out, he orders this sissy drink for two, only he doesn't realize it's for two. So the waiter shows up with this washpan of rum, and Banks is all embarrassed and so on. I told him, comics can't *get* embarrassed."

Wesley sat back down beside me and said it was time to change his life. He wanted to. "But how does a person start?"

"Small," I said. "Start small and work up. The way you would clean a house. You start in one room. Maybe you give yourself more time than you need to finish that room, just so you finish it. Then you go on to the next one. You start small, and then everything you do gets bigger."

I myself have never done it this way.

"Of course, I could be different," Wesley said. "Maybe everything I do will get smaller. On the other hand, there's still the stage, you know—when it's good up there, when I stand up there and have nothing to say but it has to work! It's—being human on purpose, it's falling back on the language in your mouth. It's facing these people and saying, You think Jesus had it rough! Ah, when it's good," he said. "And when Evie's good, too. When Evie's there. In the night. Do you know what I'm saying?" he said. "Because she's the one who is there in the night. Before her I had what you'd call contacts. Like the last one, this one that was hanging around one of the clubs—so I asked her if she'd like to go out. And she said she did. She said she wanted to go all the way out."

Wesley swallowed vodka.

"Which is something I don't even understand," he said. "How about you? Did you ever want to die? I mean, try to *make* yourself die?"

"Only once," I said. "I drove my car real fast and I was going to have an accident but then I wasn't going to."

"Well, not me, not ever," Wesley said. "I sometimes think this is how depressed the people who commit suicide get. And then I thank God I'm a Leo."

An hour before the show, Eve met us in the bar. She looked good; Wesley said so, and everyone else noticed right along with him. Marzipan skin, white-blonde hair that always looked backlit. Eve would look good in barbed wire.

"God, my jeans are full of me," Eve said, and undid a narrow snakeskin belt.

A waitress came to our table and asked what could she get us.

"I'm not drinking," Eve said. "Just a 7 UP."

The waitress asked if Sprite was okay.

"No—then make it a Tab."

"Eve here used to live next door to the vice-president

of 7 UP," Wesley explained, "so she's hip to lemon-lime drinks."

"So who's here?" Eve said. "L.A.?"

L.A. is any Hollywood agent who comes north to look at talent.

"Supposed to be, but not," Wesley said.

"It's just as well," Eve said. "They're such a tease. They fall all over you and then you never see them again." She sighed. "Just like everybody else."

She touched Wesley's shoulder, and he turned in his seat so that she could massage his neck with both hands.

"She's too good to me," Wesley said.

"Oh, I'm banking this," Eve said. "I'm not just throwing it off a cliff."

A voice broke in behind them. "Who said comedians don't have groupies."

It was the owner of the club, the man who would introduce Wesley onstage.

The owner told Wesley to join him backstage. Eve and I blew a kiss and carried our drinks upstairs. We passed people in line at the ticket window. To one side of the box office there was an eight-by-ten of Wesley. It was a publicity shot from years ago, the sincere-looking one. It was the same picture he had on his mantel at home, only there it carries a caption: "He aimed for the top. He started at the bottom. He ended up somewhere below in-between."

We found the small round table reserved for us up front. Eve offered me the first sip of her Tab so that it would be me who would get the one calorie.

"Look over there," she said, nodding far right. I

looked, and saw four men, twentyish, crowded together, a pitcher of beer on their table. They were novices who played smaller clubs on open-mike nights.

"They're something," Eve said. "Watch them when Wesley's on. When he makes you laugh, look at them. One will say, '*That's* funny,' and they'll all nod their heads madly and none of them will smile.

"A couple of months ago that little blond one opened for somebody here. He saw us in the bar after and asked Wesley what he thought of his act. Wesley said, 'Well, Bob Hope can't live forever.' The guy took it as a compliment."

Eve smiled her great rectangular smile.

I asked if she had changed her mind about Wesley, and she said, "Mmmm. Can we not talk about that?"

I worked at my drink. Eve stared at the empty stage. I said I was glad we weren't talking about *that*.

"I have a fondness for him," she said. "Sometimes it's weak. . . . Did he seem nervous to you?"

"Always."

"That's what I mean," she said. "That's why the boat. That's why," the lights went down, "I'm always here."

The owner of the club bounded onto the stage. He grabbed the microphone off its stand and began to speak. Seconds later the sound came on.

He said, "Every night I come out here and tell you what a great show we have and you know, it's the God's honest truth. But tonight I really mean it."

Eve and I scooted together till our shoulders touched. We heard him say Wesley's name. A blue spotlight fol-

lowed Wesley onstage. We heard Wesley tell the audience
how great it was to be back in L.A.

In Sydney Lawton Square, the knolls roll carefully
into each other, but the trees don't match, and there
aren't enough of them. Wesley and I pass the doggy
station—half a dozen segments of yellow-painted phone
pole carved into hydrants, to *receive* water, not give it.

"I did what she wants," Wesley says. "I got a boat,
and we're leaving the first of whatever comes after July.
Hell, I did what *I* want. I've always been a seaman at
heart—your Conrad, your Old Man and the Sea, your
fish. It'll be good to get out on the waves and sort of
expand my limitations. Sink in *water* for a change.

"As for Eve, she's not sure it will work. But it will.
I told her, The trick is this—I do what I want, and you
do what I want."

He laughs at himself. "And because, too, I love her
to death. I watch that girl like a movie. 'Eve Grant Does
Three Hours of Laundry.' I'm watching."

"Why don't you tell her these nice things?" I say.

"I could," Wesley says, doubtful. "But, hey—I guess
I'm just a jerk."

"Can you just up and go?" I say.

"I get residuals, remember—Cement cracks, this we
know. And Eve can always apply for Aid to the Totally
Disabled. You'll want to tell her I said that."

A teenage boy hefting a tape deck matched his pace
to ours and Stevie Wondered us to death.

"You know," Wesley says, as if he doesn't hear the
music, "I meet a person, and in my mind I'm saying
three minutes; I give you three minutes to show me the

spark. It's always there with Eve, and it's been how long? So I keep thinking—can't we just be together all the time whether we're together or not?"

Ahead of us poplars wave against the sky, just as if they had grown here.

"Isn't it true that that's what people can do?" Wesley asks.

And I say, "Who's to live in a world where that isn't true?" But I think, *Three popes walk into a bar.*

The Man in Bogotá

The police and emergency service people fail to make a dent. The voice of the pleading spouse does not have the hoped-for effect. The woman remains on the ledge—though not, she threatens, for long.

I imagine that I am the one who must talk the woman down. I see it, and it happens like this.

I tell the woman about a man in Bogotá. He was a wealthy man, an industrialist who was kidnapped and held for ransom. It was not a TV drama; his wife could not call the bank and, in twenty-four hours, have one million dollars. It took months. The man had a heart condition, and the kidnappers had to keep the man alive.

Listen to this, I tell the woman on the ledge. His captors made him quit smoking. They changed his diet and made him exercise every day. They held him that way for three months.

When the ransom was paid and the man was released, his doctor looked him over. He found the man to be in excellent health. I tell the woman what the doctor said then—that the kidnap was the best thing to happen to that man.

———

Maybe this is not a come-down-from-the-ledge story. But I tell it with the thought that the woman on the ledge will ask herself a question, the question that occurred to that man in Bogotá. He wondered how we know that what happens to us isn't good.

When It's Human Instead of When It's Dog

It is just inside the front door. It is the first thing she sees when she stops to wipe her feet.

It has been raining for a week, and it won't be stopping soon. It's what the people were talking about on the bus ride in, and Mrs. Hatano guesses that's what they'll be talking about on the bus ride going home.

She wonders if the stain is from water leaking in. But the plaster isn't buckled on the ceiling above the spot. It's as big as a three-quart saucepan, though it is not a perfect circle.

It is two weeks since Mrs. Hatano cleaned this house. The Mr. gave her time off after the Mrs. died. Before, Mrs. Hatano left at five o'clock. Now the schedule is this: She will come every day at five o'clock to make dinner for the Mr. She will do some light cleaning—a load of laundry, an upstairs dusting—then she will wash the dinner dishes, collect her forty dollars, and let herself out.

No one seems to be at home. Mrs. Hatano at the kitchen counter tears a sheet of paper from the telephone message pad. She draws a question mark at the top of the page. Under the question mark she writes in a column: lamb chop, pork chop, chicken, fish. She writes:

bake or broil. Vegetables she will serve cut in strips and stir-fried. The rice can cook while she runs the vacuum.

Upstairs, there is one room she never cleaned. The door was always closed, the Mrs. never well. But the door is open now.

The room is dark—the shutters are closed—so Mrs. Hatano turns on a lamp.

The wastepaper basket is filled with cards. There is an open letter on the desk, and, although it is not in Mrs. Hatano's nature to pry, she begins to read. It is a sympathy note.

Mrs. Hatano hears the front door open. She puts down the letter and moves to the bed, which is stripped of its sheets. On a chair beside the bed is a stack of clean linen, and a queen-size folded blanket.

From the doorway the Mr. says hello. He smiles at Mrs. Hatano and offers to help her make up the bed.

Before she can tell him no, he should please read his paper, the man takes two corners of the blanket and flaps it over the mattress. He waits for Mrs. Hatano to smooth out her side. She is unable to tell him, until she does, that the sheet goes first.

"My God," the man says quietly. He stares a thousand miles into the bed.

At the smell of the dinner frying in sesame oil, the man's face changes. Mrs. Hatano reads the look as Other People's Food. In the freezer she saw dinners delivered by friends—shrimp casserole, curried chicken, lasagne; the recipes were included, taped to the foil.

After serving dinner, Mrs. Hatano opens the cabinet under the sink. She removes a plastic bucket and arranges inside it a sponge, a scrub brush, a bottle of white vinegar, water, and a can of spray-on carpet cleaner.

She leaves the kitchen by the door that opens into the hall.

Mrs. Hatano sings while she works, and the foreign sounds carry to the dining room. She waters down the vinegar—so that it will not take out the color. But scrubbing the stain with vinegar fails to bring up the nap. That place on the carpet, that darker surface like geography on a map, it can still be seen.

What would do it? Mrs. Hatano says to herself.

Maybe the spray cleaner, she thinks, and points the aerosol can. She presses the button and traces the spot with foam. It must be allowed to dry, so Mrs. Hatano returns to the kitchen. She opens the freezer and takes out what's inside. She empties the crusty white ice-cube trays, and fills them with clear cold water.

While the man has his dinner, Mrs. Hatano uses the phone. She calls her friend Ruthie, who cleans down the block.

Ruthie tells her vinegar, in the first fifteen minutes. She says, "A dog wets—you can pretty much forget it. Best idea, you cut a runner from one of those carpet squares, you just cover the whole thing up."

Then Ruthie tells her it wasn't a dog. "That's where the lady died," Ruthie says. "No dogs there."

And Ruthie tells Mrs. Hatano what she heard her people say, about the day the lady died and the man carried her down the stairs.

"It happened *then*—do you hear what I'm saying?" Ruthie says.

Mrs. Hatano tries Esther Fat next. It is Esther's day off so Mrs. Hatano phones her at home.

Esther Fat says lemon and soda water. She says lemon is acid, and a stain like that is the opposite.

"Unless I am confused and it is the other way around," Esther Fat says. "Is it different when it's human instead of when it's dog?"

Mrs. Hatano thinks, What the Chinese don't know about cleaning a house.

"Hell, *they* got money," Esther Fat says. "Let them get a new rug."

When the man finishes dinner, he helps Mrs. Hatano clear the table. Then he leaves her to the dishes. That is when Mrs. Hatano sees him see the carpet.

There is no question that they see the same thing. The thin line of foam has dried to white powder, calling attention to—a state on a map? No, Mrs. Hatano thinks it looks like something else now. The white traced shape is like a chalk-drawn victim on a sidewalk.

The man excuses himself after a pause, and Mrs. Hatano washes the dishes.

When the counters are clean and the pots are put away, Mrs. Hatano gets her coat and boots. She takes the forty dollars from the table in the hall. In its place she leaves a five-dollar bill from her purse because she still could not get the spot out.

Why I'm Here

"**N**ame a time when you are happy," is one of the questions. I am taking a test to find out what to do. The way to do this is to find out what you like. This is not obvious, the way it sounds. For example, the questions that say, "Would you prefer . . ." "Would you prefer to: (a) Answer questions about what you do, (b) Answer questions about what you know, (c) Answer questions about what you think?"

My answer is, "Depends." But it's not one of the choices. I am having to think in terms of Always, Sometimes, Never.

You cannot pass or fail this test; your grade is more of a profile.

After the written part of the test, I talk to the vocational-guidance counselor. She is fifty or so, a short, square woman in a dress like a blender cozy. Mrs. Deane is the one who asks me when I'm happy. She says, "Tell me the thing you do *anyway*, and let's find a way to get you paid for that."

I ask about a job throwing sticks for dogs to fetch, and she says, "Oh, now," and gives me the courtesy laugh.

I'm the wrong age to be doing this.

You take this test in college if you can't pick a major. Or you take it to help you change your life—

later, after you've *had* a life. Somewhere in the middle is the reason why I'm here.

So—The Time When I Am Happy.

It starts with the sign that says "Open House," and the colored cellophane flags on a string across the walk. Then the unlocked door into a furnished model home, or, even better, unfurnished rooms. Here you have to imagine the lives the way you see characters in a book as you read.

It doesn't stop here, with inspecting the rooms. The thing that I do anyway—I move into new apartments.

First, I get rid of most of what I have. My friends are loaded up with ironing boards and sofa-beds. I hand out records and wicker and lamps. Never mind the plants. The books alone!

When the place is pared down, I spell my new number. It works like this: you take your telephone prefix, say it's 7-7-6. That's P-r-o. Then you start dialing words until you reach a disconnect, an available number: Pro-mise, Pro-digy, Pro-verb, Pro-blem, Pro-voke, Pro-tect, Pro-sper . . .

I buy a few beers for the "Two Guys with Van" who will load up what is left. I hope for the best, though you can count on this for damage: three moves equals a fire.

The new place brings a rush of settlement. Paper towels and spray cleaners, plastic bags to line plastic wastebaskets. There is glossy shelf paper to cut for the cabinets, and my name to put on the mailbox. It's the same thing again, three months later. Move enough times and you will never defrost a freezer.

I'm telling this to Mrs. Deane.

She says the key thing here is process—what she

looks for on the Happiness Question. Does this happiness come from a person, place, or process?

I tell her I don't know, that sometimes I just have to move.

The place before this, this is what it was. I took a small apartment on the top floor of a house. It was a narrow gray Victorian with amber stained-glass windows on the landing.

The manager apologized for the faulty showerhead. He said he would fix it, and he did—the next day. He said that he used to live in the house. He said that he and his brother used to play in my apartment where they set up their H.O. trains.

On my way out one morning, I said hello to the manager. He was down on his knees on the carpeted stairs, suctioning lint with a special vacuum attachment. But something was different when I got home that night. It took me a minute. Nothing was moved. Then I noticed the rug. It covered the space between the fireplace and couch. Since I had been gone, that rug had been vacuumed.

That wasn't all.

There was something the manager said, the day he fixed the shower. He said now that the stream was strong, I could "really lather up."

"Lather up!" I repeat to Mrs. Deane.

Mrs. Deane scans the written portion of my test. She says I skipped a question, the one that says, "Would you prefer to: (a) Think about your plans for tomorrow, (b) Think about what you would do if you had a million dollars, (c) Think about how it would feel to be held up at gunpoint?"

I say, "I want the job for the person who picks (b)."

Mrs. Deane says, "What do you suppose would happen if you just stayed put? If you just stayed still long enough to think a thing through?"

"I don't know," I say. "I won't feel like myself."

"Oh," she says, "but you will—you are."

Breathing Jesus

T hings turned around after I saw the Breathing Jesus. My lost diamond solitaire was recovered from under the couch. The orchestra noises in my head stopped warming up. My neighbor and I witnessed the Resurrection of Baby.

I had gone to Civic Center to see the Breathing Jesus. This was an *outdoor* Jesus. He was featured in the carnival they put on every springtime near the City Hall dome. An artist made this Jesus. He sat large as life on a jeweled throne in the trailer-size room that was done up as a shrine.

Out in front of the shrine was a coin box for your quarter. I dropped one in the slot, and looked at the velvet-robed figure on the throne. I watched his chest rise with the intake of air, and then fall back in the instant after someone watching beside me said, "Jesus—he's *breathing*."

I matched my respiration to the rhythm of His, and drew breath with the Lord until my quarter ran out.

I have seen a lot of things I would not know how to explain. I've seen "sparkling rain" that crackled and struck up sparks when it hit the ground. I've seen a white rainbow over the full moon. I've seen Spooklights and will-o'-the-wisps—those cold flames and luminous bubbles of light that float over swamps. I've seen a meteor wiggle out of its arc before burning itself out. I have read by the light of the southern aurora at 3 a.m.

I saw these things because of the noises in my head. Because the sound—like that of a symphony tuning up— kept me awake at night. The noises only stopped when the breath left my body and, lying there, I couldn't move.

Things happen, or they stop happening, and who can tell you why?

Baby I can explain.

Baby was only lost, not dead. But I *thought* she was dead because that is what the Department of Highways told me she was. They said a dog of Baby's description had been found at the university off-ramp. They said that the body had already been disposed of.

This was worse than it was because Baby was my neighbor's dog, left in my care while my neighbor went away.

Baby was gone three days when my neighbor returned. It was raining that day, and there was thunder, too. I felt strangely calm, prepared to deliver the news. I felt lucky to have my wits about me, and worried that I might need them.

And then there was Baby before I had to say.

What brought her back from where she was could have been the tires on the gravel drive. Or maybe it was the thunderstorm, the first one of the season, with the low and rolling sounds that wake up those in hibernation.

If that wasn't it, then I don't know what was.

I don't know why the breathing stops. They don't know why you get it, and they can't make it go away. There's a name for when the breathing stops, and they think that it's the killer when those babies die in their cribs.

I'm careful going to sleep at night. Always there is the noise before I can't get air. What I do is put a sound there first, the sound of someone else's breathing, regular and deep. At night I am back in the carnival tent, breathing along with Jesus. It's—in with the good air, then out with the same good air, breathing with something that can't breathe by itself.

I breathe along with Jesus till my quarter runs out, until I run out of change and take up a dollar bill from my purse. In my mind I say to anyone, Give me change for a dollar? Can you get me another four quarters?

Because you have to believe that something will work. I don't, but you have got to.

The ticking of a clock is what does the trick for Baby.

The things I've seen I can't explain are nothing next to what I've heard—musical sand, whispering lakes, a shout whose echo came back as a song.

Oh, I've heard stranger things than that, but those were in my head.

Today Will Be
a Quiet Day

think it's the other way around," the boy said. "I think if the quake hit now the *bridge* would collapse and the *ramps* would be left."

He looked at his sister with satisfaction.

"You are just trying to scare your sister," the father said. "You know that is not true."

"No, really," the boy insisted, "and I heard birds in the middle of the night. Isn't that a warning?"

The girl gave her brother a toxic look and ate a handful of Raisinets. The three of them were stalled in traffic on the Golden Gate Bridge.

That morning, before waking his children, the father had canceled their music lessons and decided to make a day of it. He wanted to know how they were, is all. Just —how were they. He thought his kids were as self-contained as one of those dogs you sometimes see carrying home its own leash. But you could read things wrong.

Could you ever.

The boy had a friend who jumped from a floor of Langley Porter. The friend had been there for two weeks, mostly playing Ping-Pong. All the friend said the day the boy visited and lost every game was never play Ping-Pong with a mental patient because it's all we do and we'll kill you. That night the friend had cut the red belt he wore in two and left the other half on his bed.

That was this time last year when the boy was twelve
years old.

You think you're safe, the father thought, but it's
thinking you're invisible because you closed your eyes.

This day they were headed for Petaluma—the chicken,
egg, and arm-wrestling capital of the nation—for lunch.
The father had offered to take them to the men's arm-
wrestling semifinals. But it was said that arm-wrestling
wasn't so interesting since the new safety precautions,
that hardly anyone broke an arm or a wrist anymore.
The best anyone could hope to see would be dislocation,
so they said they would rather go to Pete's. Pete's was
a gas station turned into a place to eat. The hamburgers
there were named after cars, and the gas pumps in front
still pumped gas.

"Can I have one?" the boy asked, meaning the
Raisinets.

"No," his sister said.

"Can I have two?"

"Neither of you should be eating candy before lunch,"
the father said. He said it with the good sport of a father
who enjoys his kids and gets a kick out of saying Dad
things.

"You mean dinner," said the girl. "It will be dinner
before we get to Pete's."

Only the northbound lanes were stopped. Southbound
traffic flashed past at the normal speed.

"Check it out," the boy said from the back seat. "Did

you see the bumper sticker on that Porsche? 'If you don't like the way I drive, stay off the sidewalk.'"

He spoke directly to his sister. "I've just solved my Christmas shopping."

"I got the highest score in my class in Driver's Ed," she said.

"I thought I would let your sister drive home today," the father said.

From the back seat came sirens, screams for help, and then a dirge.

The girl spoke to her father in a voice rich with complicity. "Don't people make you want to give up?"

"Don't the two of you know any jokes? I haven't laughed all day," the father said.

"Did I tell you the guillotine joke?" the girl said.

"He hasn't laughed all day, so you must've," her brother said.

The girl gave her brother a look you could iron clothes with. Then her gaze dropped down. "Oh-oh," she said, "Johnny's out of jail."

Her brother zipped his pants back up. He said, "Tell the joke."

"Two Frenchmen and a Belgian were about to be beheaded," the girl began. "The first Frenchman was led to the block and blindfolded. The executioner let the blade go. But it stopped a quarter inch above the Frenchman's neck. So he was allowed to go free, and ran off shouting, '*C'est un miracle! C'est un miracle!*'"

"What does that mean?" her brother asked.

"It's a miracle," the father said.

"Then the second Frenchman was led to the block, and same thing—the blade stopped just before cutting off his head. So *he* got to go free, and ran off shouting '*C'est un miracle!*'

"Finally the Belgian was led to the block. But before they could blindfold him, he looked up, pointed to the guillotine, and cried, '*Voilà la difficulté!*' "

She doubled over.

"Maybe *I* would be wetting *my* pants if I knew what that meant," the boy said.

"You can't explain after the punchline," the girl said, "and have it still be funny."

"There's the problem," said the father.

The waitress handed out menus to the party of three seated in the corner booth of what used to be the lube bay. She told them the specialty of the day was Moroccan chicken.

"That's what I want," the boy said, "Morerotten chicken."

But he changed his order to a Studeburger and fries after his father and sister had ordered.

"So," the father said, "who misses music lessons?"

"I'm serious about what I asked you last week," the girl said. "About switching to piano? My teacher says a real flutist only breathes with the stomach, and I can't."

"The real reason she wants to change," said the boy, "is her waist will get two inches bigger when she learns to stomach-breathe. That's what *else* her teacher said."

The boy buttered a piece of sourdough bread and flipped a chunk of cold butter onto his sister's sleeve.

"Jeezo-beezo," the girl said, "why don't they skip the knife and fork and just set his place with a slingshot!"

"Who will ever adopt you if you don't mind your manners?" the father said. "Maybe we could try a little quiet today."

"You sound like your tombstone," the girl said. "Remember what you wanted it to say?"

Her brother joined in with his mouth full: "Today will be a quiet day."

"Because it never is with us around," the boy said.

"You guys," said the father.

The waitress brought plates. The father passed sugar to the boy and salt to the girl without being asked. He watched the girl shake out salt onto the fries.

"If I had a sore throat, I would gargle with those," he said.

"Looks like she's trying to melt a driveway," the boy offered.

The father watched his children eat. They ate fast. They called it Hoovering. He finished while they sucked at straws in empty drinks.

"Funny," he said thoughtfully, "I'm not hungry anymore."

Every meal ended this way. It was his benediction, one of the Dad things they expected him to say.

"That reminds me," the girl said. "Did you feed Rocky before we left?"

"Uh-uh," her brother said. "I fed him yesterday."

"*I* fed him yesterday!" the girl said.

"Okay, we'll compromise," the boy said. "We won't feed the cat today."

"I'd say you are out of bounds on that one," the father
said.

He meant you could not tease her about animals.
Once, during dinner, that cat ran into the dining room
shot from guns. He ran around the table at top speed,
then spun out on the parquet floor into a leg of the table.
He fell onto his side and made short coughing sounds.
"Isn't he smart?" the girl had crooned, kneeling beside
him. "He knows he's hurt."

For years, her father had to say that the animals seen
on shoulders of roads were napping.

"He never would have not fed Homer," she said to
her father.

"Homer was a dog," the boy said. "If I forgot to feed
him, he could just go into the hills and bite a deer."

"Or a Campfire Girl selling candy at the front door,"
their father reminded them.

"Homer," the girl sighed. "I hope he likes chasing
sheep on that ranch in the mountains."

The boy looked at her, incredulous.

"You *believed* that? You actually *believed* that?"

In her head, a clumsy magician yanked the cloth and
the dishes all crashed to the floor. She took air into her
lungs until they filled, and then she filled her stomach,
too.

"I thought she knew," the boy said.

The dog was five years ago.

"The girl's parents insisted," the father said. "It's the
law in California."

"Then I hate California," she said. "I hate its guts."

The boy said he would wait for them in the car, and left the table.

"What would help?" the father asked.

"For Homer to be alive," she said.

"What would help?"

"Nothing."

"Help."

She pinched a trail of salt on her plate.

"A ride," she said. "I'll drive."

The girl started the car and screamed. "Goddammit!"

With the power off, the boy had tuned in the Spanish station. Mariachis exploded on ignition.

"Dammit isn't God's last name," the boy said, quoting another bumper sticker.

"Don't people make you want to give up?" the father said.

"No talking," the girl said to the rearview mirror, and put the car in gear.

She drove for hours. Through groves of eucalyptus with their damp peeling bark, past acacia bushes with yellow flowers pulsing off their stems. She cut over to the coast route and the stony gray-green tones of Inverness.

"What you'd call scenic," the boy tried.

Otherwise, they were quiet.

No one said anything else until the sky started to close, and then it was the boy again, asking shouldn't they be going home.

"No, no," the father said, and made a show of looking out the window, up at the sky and back at his watch. "No," he said, "keep driving—it's getting earlier."

But the sky spilled rain, and the girl headed south towards the bridge. She turned on the headlights and the dashboard lit up green. She read off the odometer on the way home: "Twenty-six thousand, three hundred eighty-three and eight-tenths miles."

"Today?" the boy said.

The boy got to Rocky first. "Let's play the cat," he said, and carried the Siamese to the upright piano. He sat on the bench holding the cat in his lap and pressed its paws to the keys. Rocky played "Born Free." He tried to twist away.

"Come on, Rocky, ten more minutes and we'll break."

"Give him to me," the girl said.

She puckered up and gave the cat a five-lipper.

"Bring the Rock upstairs," the father called. "Bring sleeping bags, too."

Pretty soon three sleeping bags formed a triangle in the master bedroom. The father was the hypotenuse. The girl asked him to brush out her hair, which he did while the boy ate a tangerine, peeling it up close to his face, inhaling the mist. Then he held each segment to the light to find seeds. In his lap, cat paws fluttered like dreaming eyes.

"What are you thinking?" the father asked.

"Me?" the girl said. "Fifty-seven T-bird, white with red interior, convertible. I drive it to Texas and wear skirts with rick-rack. I'm changing my name to Ruby," she said, "or else Easy."

The father considered her dream of a checkered future.

"Early ripe, early rot," he warned.

A wet wind slammed the window in its warped sash, and the boy jumped.

"I hate rain," he said. "I hate its guts."

The father got up and closed the window tighter against the storm. "It's a real frog-choker," he said.

In darkness, lying still, it was no less camplike than if they had been under the stars singing to a stone-ringed fire burned down to embers.

They had already said good-night some minutes earlier when the boy and girl heard their father's voice in the dark.

"Kids, I just remembered—I have some good news and some bad news. Which do you want first?"

It was his daughter who spoke. "Let's get it over with," she said. "Let's get the bad news over with."

The father smiled. They are all right, he decided. My kids are as right as this rain. He smiled at the exact spots he knew their heads were turned to his, and doubted he would ever feel—not better, but *more* than he did now.

"I lied," he said. "There is no bad news."